This Winnie-the-Pooh
book belongs to:

....

EGMONT

We bring stories to life

First published in Great Britain 2013
by Egmont UK Limited, The Yellow Building, 1 Nicholas Road, London W11 4AN
www.egmont.co.uk

Illustrated by Andrew Grey
Based on the 'Winnie-the-Pooh' works by A.A.Milne and E.H.Shepard
Illustrations © 2013 Disney Enterprises Inc.

ISBN 978 1 4052 6748 9

A CIP catalogue record for this title is available from the British Library.

Stay safe online. Any website addresses listed in this book are correct at the time of going to print.
However, Egmont is not responsible for content hosted by third parties. Please be aware that
online content can be subject to change and websites can contain content that is unsuitable for
children. We advise that all children are supervised when using the internet.

Egmont is passionate about helping to preserve the world's remaining ancient forests.
We only use paper from legal and sustainable forest sources.

This book is made from paper certified by the Forest Stewardship Council® (FSC),
an organisation dedicated to promoting responsible management of forest resources.
For more information on the FSC, please visit www.fsc.org. To learn more about
Egmont's sustainable paper policy, please visit www.egmont.co.uk/ethical.

Winnie-the-Pooh

Pooh's Christmas Letters

EGMONT

One cold morning, Pooh was strolling through the Hundred Acre Wood...

. . . and humming
a little hum to himself
when he had an idea.
It was a good idea.
A CHRISTMASSY idea.

The next morning Piglet woke up to find a letter on his doorstep.

"Please come to the North Pole at lunchtime. Signed, a Friend," it said.

Piglet was confused. Who could have written it?

Piglet decided to take the letter to Pooh.
Even though Pooh was a Bear of Very Little
Brain, he might know who had written it.

B ut when Piglet got to Pooh's house, Pooh wasn't there.

"Hello Piglet," said Christopher Robin, stomping through the snow in his wellington boots. "Where's Winnie-the-Pooh?"

Piglet explained that he didn't know. "I've had a letter, Christopher Robin," he said.

"May I see it, please?" asked Christopher Robin. After he had read it he thought for a moment and said, "I'd better go to the North Pole. You fetch the others, Piglet, and meet me there . . ."

Piglet went straight to Kanga's house. They had had a letter too!

"Merry Christmas," it said. "Come to the North Pole for lunch. A Friend."

Tigger and Roo were very excited. They couldn't wait to get going. But Kanga was cautious. "Let's go and see Rabbit – he always knows what to do," she said.

On the other side of the forest, Eeyore and Owl had also received a letter. "If you come to the North Pole I will reveal my surprise," it said.

"Oh," said Eeyore gloomily, "I thought it might have been something important."

"Most curious," said Owl. "I believe we ought to consult Rabbit." And off they went, through the deep snow, to Rabbit's house.

They arrived at the same time as Kanga, Roo and Tigger. Rabbit was reading a letter that had come through his door that morning.

"Happy Christmas! Tiddley Pom!" he read. "Hurry to the North Pole for a surprise luncheon!"

"I believe," said Rabbit, "that if we go to the North Pole, we shall find out who has written these mysterious letters."

So they all set off through the crunchy snow to the North Pole. Rabbit led the way, and all the other friends followed behind him.

"I hope a HEFFALUMP didn't write the letters," said Piglet anxiously.

Soon they arrived at the North Pole, and there, waiting for them, were Christopher Robin and Winnie-the-Pooh!

"Happy Christmas!" cried Pooh. "It was me who sent you all the letters! And there's one letter left."

Christopher Robin read the last letter aloud. It was a Christmas card to all his friends.

"Welcome to my surprise Christmas Luncheon," it read. "There's plenty for everyone!"

And so they all sat down to eat their Christmas Lunch, organised by their dear friend, Pooh Bear. Everyone had a wonderful time – even Eeyore!

Enjoy more wintry tales
with Winnie-the-Pooh and friends!

Winnie-the-Pooh
Pooh's Snowy Day

ISBN 978 1 4052 5775 6

Winnie-the-Pooh
Pooh's Christmas Adventure

ISBN 978 1 4052 6282 8